CW00923443

Tomorrow, When I Was Young

Julie Travis

Tomorrow When I Was young by Julie Travis

ISBN: 978-1-908125-87-3

Cover Art by David Rix

Publication Date: October 2019

All text copyright 2019 Julie Travis

To the women who saved me from drowning.

"There are many ways to contact the dead. This is just one of them."

So said The Golden Sea Captain as they docked. The city was only accessible to the living during the Serpent Moon, which occurred each twelve and a quarter years. Zanders nodded as she always did, trying to appear wise, and secured the ropes. The ship, a beautiful, three-masted clipper, had arrived safely despite having no crew that she was aware of. Together they left the harbour and explored the city.

Kensal was a necropolis in the true sense of the term. Zanders had visited many great cemeteries over the years, awed at the huge monuments they contained, but had found it ironic that these wonderful buildings contained only coffins, or marked the place of a burial. This, then, was her perfect city of the dead; one where the mausoleums were occupied by families of living corpses. Each building looked as it would in a cemetery, with a plaque or inscription on the outside, giving the names and dates of death of the occupants, often with an elaborate description of their achievements during their lifetimes, but they were homes to the dead, who went about their business much the same as the living did, it appeared. Outside one especially grand mausoleum sat an elderly woman on a simple wooden chair, cradling a baby in her arms. The tall metal doors had been propped open to let a little light and air inside. Zanders caught the scent of damp as she passed by but, despite slowing down, could not see inside. Instead she glanced at the old woman, who returned her gaze. It was a chilling moment for both of them, each realising the difference of the other. The old woman looked appalling – well preserved but with skin the shade of candlewax and features that had lost the use of muscles to give her any expression. Zanders avoided looking at the baby; it was likely to be a distressing sight. The Golden Sea Captain gave Zanders' shoulder a gentle squeeze.

"Don't draw attention to yourself. To us. We are barely tolerated here as it is."

Zanders wondered why that was, whether it was down to their being living, breathing people, or to The Golden Sea Captain's strange appearance. On boarding the ship, Zanders had realised almost immediately that the fierce-looking Captain was not the man he portrayed himself as. Did anyone else see it? Perhaps not. Zanders had read of women throughout history dressing as men in order to go to sea or to war, or to pursue the love of their life if that love happened to be female – but to be with one of these women, to be *inside* history, was as exciting as it was disconcerting. Zanders had nearly slipped up in conversation in various ports and had decided to refer to The Golden Sea Captain as *the Captain* rather than using any gender-specific terms. It sometimes made her conversation a little clumsy but was safer for both of them.

The Captain proffered an arm and it felt natural to take it as they walked. At some point – no doubt during their travels on the empty ship – Zanders would pluck up the courage to find out everything there was to know about The Golden Sea Captain but for now, there were only the avenues of the dead to walk, as unselfconsciously as possible, without crying or asking prying questions. Besides, the Captain was not judging *her*. Zanders had no idea how she'd boarded The Giantess; she had simply been sleeping in a chair at home and had awoken in the Captain's bed, with him sitting nearby, wearing what was supposed to be a stern expression.

And now, after all their travels, they were here. Zanders felt reassured that she had a uniformed Sea Captain with her. These were the days when such authority was respected, so they would be safer than if they were simply two women walking through the city. Zanders noted each family name as casually as she could, although the fact that she and the Captain were clearly different to the city's residents was reassuring – it confirmed that she was, at least, still alive and this bizarre adventure was not a post-death experience.

Life before she'd arrived on The Giantess had become a series of tragedies. Zanders had lost parents, lovers, aunts and friends. *Lost*, of course, was the wrong word, a word to anaesthetise the fact that they had all died. It was she who was lost. In a material sense, life was also a tragedy, but it was one that was more easily understood; disabled by having several vertebrae crushed, and having sold everything she could bear to get rid of, she'd realised that hardship and the judgement of strangers were just additional elements of her disability. Needing to connect with the snippets of the history her grandmother had given her – of an ancestor from Peru – she had turned to the Internet and genealogy websites. They had turned up very little before demanding money but in a box given to her by her one remaining aunt was a bundle of old photographs. One showed a group of people on a mountain plateau, the women dressed in shawls and what looked like tall bowler hats. The second was a portrait of one of the women from the group photograph. The woman was dressed more formally, sitting at a table and staring, unsmiling, at the camera. The group photo was far more cheerful, but the second one showed the woman's face more clearly. Zanders' aunt knew nothing about the photos, hadn't even looked through them in years, but she remembered the inscription on the back of the portrait when Zanders read it to her over the phone.

At her new home, Salcombe.

"Salcombe was the family home for years. It was a wonderful place, so I heard. We weren't always poor, you see. Your grandmother would have written that inscription. She was always trying to put things in order."

The photograph sparked Zanders' imagination and when her aunt died a few months later, she found herself desperate to find out more about the mysterious Peruvian woman in her family.

"Found anyone you know? Family? Friends?"

They had stopped on a corner, The Golden Sea Captain smoking a cigarette while Zanders spoke to more of the residents and showed them the portrait. She had been as discreet as possible and the Captain noted that no one seemed agitated by the stranger asking questions. The Captain was still slightly nervous, but found nervousness a good state to be in. It was more conducive to staying alive.

Zanders was also nervous. She had never met the dead before and wasn't sure how to act around them. She was also worried about what they would look like close up. On the edge of the necropolis, at the beginning of their exploration, she had just wanted to cry but by the time they were halfway round, she was used to their appearance. Those who'd experienced violent deaths had been stitched up, open fractures repaired, skull fragments carefully replaced. Contrary to Zanders' first impression, they all bore a weary expression. She was not surprised – death was bound to give a person a particular view of the world. But the people she spoke to were friendly, although none recognised the woman in the photograph. Zanders stood on the threshold of one of the mausoleums, talking to some of the occupants. One, a young man with a bullet hole in his cheek, studied the photograph a second time.

"I don't know her, Madame," he said, "although there are many people here. What is her name? When did she pass over?"

"All I have is the photo, I'm afraid," said Zanders. "And that she moved from Peru to Salcombe, on the South Coast of England."

Before Zanders moved away, she looked past the young man into his home. Again, the overwhelming impression was of dark and damp. She berated herself for her relief at not being able to smell the decay.

"No luck here," Zanders said, in reply to The Golden Sea Captain's question. "No one recognised the photograph. How many places are there like this? I could be looking forever."

They returned to The Giantess. The tide wouldn't be right to set sail until the morning. Zanders was tired but not overwhelmed by it; her crushed spine had not affected her since she'd arrived on the ship. However she had got here, she knew she was awake and alive, and she blessed her return to health. The ship was silent, as ever, and Zanders found it both peaceful and eerie. The absence of a crew meant that she felt more able to wander around, but she also wondered whether she was surrounded by ghosts – The Golden Sea Captain could not possibly sail the ship alone. The Giantess, however, was no ordinary ship. Zanders had realised this as soon as she'd seen the figurehead. The Giantess was a monstrous woman. She held none of the conventional beauty of other figureheads, but was instead a furious, naked warning to any who tried to attack her, be they human, or storm, or sea monster. She stood upon a small wooden platform, staring intently at the sea. It was comforting.

After dinner they sat on the deck, enjoying the sunset. Each had questions for the other but stayed silent, not knowing where to start and not wanting to spoil the evening. The Golden Sea Captain stood up suddenly and peered out into the gloom. Zanders followed suit and saw a figure running down the quay towards them. It was the young man with the bullet wound on his face.

"Captain! Madame!" he called softly as he drew level. "I found two people who remembered the lady you're looking for."

It was still light enough for the young man to see their expressions and the eagerness on Zanders' face showed the bargaining power he might have.

"Take me with you and I'll tell you everything," he said.

Zanders heard The Golden Sea Captain sigh. "I cannot do that. You cannot leave Kensal," he said.

Zanders was about to ask why when the young man gave a desperate wail.

"*S'il vous plait!* I must return to the Land Of The Living. I can't spend any longer here. I'll stay hidden. I'll do any work you want."

The Golden Sea Captain shook his head. "If it was up to me I'd take you. But it's not physically possible. The sea would take you – wherever you hid – and bring you back here."

Zanders wept at the dismay on the young man's face; he knew the Captain was right, but had been hoping for a miracle.

"I'm sorry," said the Captain. "I wish it were different. If you have some information, then

I'd ask you to tell us. Miss Zanders dearly needs to find her ancestor."

The young man stood quietly, deciding what to do – and Zanders wondered what she would do in the same situation.

He decided to be honourable rather than punish her.

"After you left, I asked some of my older neighbours if they knew of the woman. One couple recognised the description I gave them. They met her in life."

Zanders was transfixed. Then she remembered her manners and held up the bottle of sherry they'd been drinking. The young man shook his head and continued.

"Her name is Lorena Alvarez. She was a nice woman, but unhappy in England."

The Golden Sea Captain considered this. "Miss Zanders wishes to contact her. How would she go about such a thing? Is Mrs Alvarez likely to be close to her place of burial?"

The young man shrugged. "It's possible. Although perhaps not if she was buried in England. She may have returned to her family's village."

"Which village is that?" asked Zanders.

"Take me with you," pleaded the young man one last time, in a tone that knew it was impossible. Then, with a desperate burst of energy, he leapt towards The Giantess and clung onto one of the mooring ropes. But before he could make his way towards the ship, a wave reared up and took him.

Zanders screamed and bent as far as she could over the side. The Golden Sea Captain put an arm around her shoulder to steady her, and whispered in her ear.

"He won't drown. That's the tragedy. He'll be washed up on the beach and be all the sadder for it."

They searched the little harbour beach until it was too dark to see, but there was no sign of the young man. The Golden Sea Captain looked pensive as they boarded The Giantess.

"It would be best to set sail now, but the tide's too low. I wonder if our presence here is going to cause trouble."

"I feel terrible about that poor man. God knows what he's going through because of me."

"This isn't your fault. He was unhappy at being dead long before we arrived, just as some of the living are miserable with their state of being. No one here seemed to resent us visiting, but I'm not sure how they'll take two of the living staying here all night, especially now. No matter, it can't be helped. I have a rifle and a pistol in my cabin and a barricade for the door. I think you'd be safer with me tonight."

Zanders was surprised at the suggestion. She'd assumed the Captain would not take the risk of revealing his gender, but he remained dressed in trousers and shirt as he lay in bed – in readiness, he said, should there be an attack on the ship. He kissed her cheek goodnight and Zanders fell asleep, still sad at the young man's despair but feeling safe and secure.

Something Zanders had been aware of when she'd got over the shock of her sudden arrival on The Giantess was The Golden Sea Captain's enthusiasm – and, it seemed, relief – that a mission had been suggested. The Captain had not interrogated her about why she was on board. The questions he'd asked had been out of genuine interest rather than a demand for information; despite his military uniform, he was clearly not part of the British Navy. Where they were in the world was something The Golden Sea Captain didn't appear to be aware of. Maps and charts covered the huge table in the Captain's office but when asked for their position he just said, "We are between here and there."

But now, safely away from the city of the dead, Zanders wondered whether the Captain had been vague or whether *Here* and *There* actually existed. Anything seemed possible at the moment. The Captain, too, seemed to be easily passing as male. Zanders had the luxury of her 21st Century knowledge of history to see what others did not, although it had occurred to her that, given their cultural differences, the dead may have simply not cared – perhaps it was amongst the living where the Captain was most in danger. Looking at the Captain now Zanders realised what a handsome man this woman was. She brushed the thought away and stood beside the Captain at the wheel.

"Where are we going next?"

The Captain looked at her. "Peru would be the logical place. We now have your ancestor's name. If we are to assume she was buried at Salcombe, where she was apparently unhappy, her spirit is likely to be closer to us in her home village than there."

"But where in Peru?" asked Zanders. "There must be hundreds of mountain villages."

"There are people who can help," said The Golden Sea Captain. "Shamen, wise women, magicians. If we become desperate, we can even try Government officials," he said, smiling. "Between the conventional and the unconventional, we'll find her. Or her family. I'm sure of it."

The charts showed that The Giantess was now sailing in known waters. Peru was some distance away but they had information now, a purpose. To visit Lorena Alvarez' village – her family, even – was more than Zanders could ever have hoped for.

While Zanders was below decks, gazing at the charts, The Golden Sea Captain ordered one of the ghost crew to take the wheel. Over his years as a Captain, he had found ghosts to make the best crew. They didn't question orders or mutiny; they had no need for precious food and water supplies. Or rest, for that matter. They'd spent their lives at sea and knew nothing else. Working on the ship was the closest they came to being at rest.

The Captain looked over the side of the ship, into the Pacific. Conditions were almost perfect; the wind up enough to make good progress, the waves small enough not to impede them. The Captain found the ocean endlessly fascinating and frightening. To not be able to see far below the surface stirred his imagination – there could be whales swimming underneath the ship right now and should one of them surface at the wrong time, The Giantess could be tipped over or broken in half. Even bigger creatures could be lurking – gigantic squid were said to have brought down several ships in the area in deliberate attacks. But all the Captain could see was blue darkness, punctuated by jellyfish a yard in diameter.

The arrival of Zanders – who would not say how she'd managed to stowaway and remain undiscovered for so long (he assumed she'd sneaked aboard on one of his stops, in the Mediterranean, perhaps) – had caused some disruption but she was now a welcome addition. The mission to find her family was a noble one. The Golden Sea Captain was determined to succeed and they'd been lucky so far – the occurrence of the Serpent Moon had been perfect; Kensal had provided some vital information. Zanders, in her odd clothing and in the way she moved and spoke, was like no Englishwoman the Captain had ever seen. He was becoming tempted, though, to believe her story – that she had fallen asleep at home and woken up on The Giantess. Strange things happened, and Zanders' need to connect with her past may have triggered such an event.

There was time, now, to talk; The Golden Sea Captain estimated that they would reach the coast of Peru within the month, if all went well. And it did, although it was not uneventful; for a while, a gigantic squid followed, directly behind the ship. Zanders was elated to see a creature she'd thought of as mythological. The beast was huge, perhaps three times the length of The Giantess. The Golden Sea Captain was far less enthusiastic at its appearance and had his guns loaded and ready should it attack. When the creature disappeared, he blew a kiss at the ship's figurehead for protecting them once again.

Little by little Zanders talked about her life and the 160 years between them. She reckoned that a Sea Captain who knew how to contact the dead should be able to cope with the concept of her waking up in a different time and place to where she'd fallen asleep. And he *was* able to consider it, frowning and mulling it over but never dismissing it.

"Do you want to know what the future looks like?" she asked him.

The Golden Sea Captain's eyes widened in horror. "No! It cannot be right for me to know."

Zanders admired the Captain's restraint. But it was an alarming thought. It made her wonder if there would be repercussions – to her future self or the time she was in now – from her being here.

Now was the time for asking questions, though, so she took the opportunity.

"Is there anything you want to tell me? About yourself?"

The Golden Sea Captain chose his words very carefully.

"Being a man affords privileges, many privileges that females do not get. It opens doors. Provides safe passage. Gives one's words gravitas. And allows for more unrestricted behaviour. Men don't see these as privileges; they assume they are rights. Perhaps the world would be different – improved – if they could see this from the outside."

There was no need to say more, so he fell silent. And Zanders realised The Golden Sea Captain was as displaced as she was.

After her parents had died, Zanders was struck by a memory of a childhood holiday, of walking up a dusty lane in boiling heat and finding a small merry-go-round by the roadside. Zanders had ridden on it every day that week, sitting on the top deck of the miniature omnibus, never questioning why she was the only passenger, or why a solitary merry-go-round would be in such a deserted area. Eventually she wondered whether it was a memory or a dream. The past was crumbling around her. Would it one day be that none of it had ever happened, that her whole life was just a series of dreams? Zanders had tried to protect herself from grief, to cushion its blows, but there was no armour in existence strong enough to keep its wearer safe. Grief still managed to crush her heart and send her into freefall.

The only way forward, it seemed, was to retreat to the past. If Zanders could find the details of her mysterious ancestor's life, it would provide her with an anchor, something from her family's history that she'd know was fact. On the day she'd disappeared, she'd been unable to go out, her injury wracking every part of her body with pain.

It was the loneliest of days but somehow she'd escaped. Whether she'd return was something that had barely crossed her mind.

Mollendo, the southernmost port in Peru, was busy. Alive. So much so that Zanders was nervous about leaving the safety of The Giantess. She had shared the ship with ghosts and had explored a city of the dead; the vitality of crowds of the living was something she was no longer used to. However, The Golden Sea Captain left the ghost crew carrying out repairs and accompanied Zanders through the town. He had paid for information as to who to get information from, and so they left Mollendo – much to Zanders' relief – and headed a short distance towards the towering rise of the Andes. On the edge of a wood stood a house, although it took them a while to recognise it as such. Two trees had entwined, growing together over the course of decades. The trunks began vertically, then had slowly pulled each other over so that they were heading horizontally further into the wood. Branches had been manipulated to frame a long, single-storey space, with the leaves providing a roof. The house was an extension, a lovechild, of the embracing trees.

This was the home of the *Mujer de Aves* – the Bird Woman, The Golden Sea Captain explained. She was a herbalist, wise woman and witch, and held in reverence by the local people, who came to her with many questions. The *Mujer de Aves* was their best hope for information about Lorena Alvarez.

The Golden Sea Captain was about to announce their presence when the door, fashioned from dead tree trunks, opened and the Bird Woman appeared. Zanders chided herself for expecting a wizened old woman, a cartoon of a witch; the Bird Woman was younger than herself – in her mid-30s, Zanders guessed – and quite strikingly beautiful. She tied her hair back and held up a hand in a strange gesture of welcome.

The Golden Sea Captain spoke to her in Spanish for a few moments, then the Bird Woman nodded.

"I speak enough English for you," she said, raising her arm a little higher. Her shawl slipped off her arm, revealing tiny, stubbly feathers – or tattoos of feathers. The woman's hand, open, palm up, began to melt. A drop stretched and fell from her fingers. Zanders covered her mouth to stop from screaming and gasped with relief when The Golden Sea Captain murmured, *"Honey"*. There was movement among the trees and a pair of hummingbirds appeared. They were the most amazing birds Zanders had ever seen; their bodies seemed to be made of green metal and they had bright yellow wings and yellow bands around their necks. Their heads were hooded with shining black feathers and huge eyes peered at the Bird

Woman's dripping hand. They hovered close by, tongues flicking from long beaks, lapping up the offered feast.

The Bird Woman gazed at the hummingbirds as she addressed Zanders.

"I see you have Death around you, circling, the loss of those you loved. You loved them so dearly that you thought it would protect them but they died anyway and you thought it was because your love wasn't strong enough to save them. And so your world and your body fell apart – you had no option but to come here."

Zanders was impressed, although she was aware her body language could tell an observant person all of these things.

The Bird Woman beckoned with her free hand. "You need to build up your strength," she said. "Come, take some honey."

And Zanders stood alongside the hummingbirds and lapped honey from the witch's hand.

Later, they sat in the Bird Woman's house. The Golden Sea Captain had left them on the Bird Woman's instruction and returned to The Giantess. Zanders was sprawling rather than sitting, having chewed the dried fungus the Bird Woman had given her. The Bird Woman smoked a pipe of what

Zanders supposed was a more potent version of the same thing. The effect on Zanders was profound enough – the photo of Lorena Alvarez that she'd shown now had more depth and there was life in it – a little dog was now sitting on the woman's lap, and the woman looked less solemn – but the effect on the Bird Woman was astounding. The tiny feathers – clearly not tattoos – grew, covering her arms and neck up to her jawline. She spoke and sang in Spanish for a while, smiling benevolently at Zanders, who could only lie there as a carpet of purple flowers grew underneath and around her. Convinced it was a hallucination, she brushed her fingers through them and to her surprise, they came away pollen-stained. She looked up at the Bird Woman as she sat, smoke surrounding her like a captivated audience. Her nose had been replaced by a long, dark beak; her eyes were big and round and saw everything. Zanders, nauseous with motion sickness, lay back in the flowers and took in their sickly scent. Did any trace of her remain at home? Had she disappeared completely there; was anyone searching for her? She had a vision of an imprint of herself lying in her bed, a carbon copy that faded by the hour. Was she missed, as she missed others so much? Or had Time there stopped, awaiting her return? She wanted to talk to the Bird Woman, who would know the answers to these questions, but Zanders was as incapable of asking as the Bird Woman was of replying – in human language, anyway. It was possible, however, that at some point the following conversation took place:

"How is it that I'm here?" asked Zanders.

"Time is not a straight line. The past, the present and the future run in parallel. You have stepped from one to another. It is not so unusual to do so," said the Bird Woman, who was quite easy to understand, despite having a beak.

"Will I return to the present?"

"You are already in the present. Where you came from is now the future. Do you see how fluid these things are?" the Bird Woman replied.

It was suddenly clear. Zanders' own past was now also the future. Where she was now would only become the past again if she returned to where she'd come from – or to anywhere else in the future to now.

"I would think," continued the Bird Woman, "that you would be able to find a way to return, once you've done what you need to do here. The real question is – do you wish to return?"

That was a question Zanders could not answer.

It was all real, Zanders finally decided, when The Golden Sea Captain returned and caught sight of the Bird Woman's feathers. By then she was leading Zanders in a dance around the house. Both were grateful to see that the Captain had brought a bottle of wine with him. The Bird Woman drank two cupfuls and then revealed what she knew.

"Lorena Alvarez lived at Tierra de Flores, a hundred miles to the north-west, high in the mountains. I was able to fly there. Her spirit roams this beautiful village. Her family is still there. It is a difficult life for them. As it is for all of us, each in our own way," she said, regarding each of them pointedly.

As they got ready to leave, the Bird Woman clasped Zanders in her feathery arms.

"I could make you a potion that would stop you *feeling*. No more grief. No more loneliness. But you would die inside."

"I'm dead inside now," said Zanders.

The Bird Woman held her face. "No! That is the pain of life. Of love. It is unbearable. But we must experience it, for the alternative is infinitely worse. I have used the potion only twice in my eighty years, and it is not for you."

They said their goodbyes and the Captain gave the Bird Woman her fee. It was only when they had left the wood that Zanders fully comprehended how old the Bird Woman really was.

The Golden Sea Captain stood naked in front of the mirror. It was a transformation that verged on the magical, she thought, to strip off the clothing that made her a distinguished Sea Captain, a man of authority, and become a shapely, vulnerable woman. She sometimes forgot that she was female – when The Giantess was crashing through a storm, or when the barmaid at an inn blushed when he spoke to her. When she saw doors opening, respect being given, because of her gender, she gratefully hid behind the façade she'd created, but she never wished to *be* male. She loved her body, her Self, just as she was. She'd guessed the Bird Woman would see behind the disguise, but had her strange guest? Zanders had hinted that she did – and The Golden Sea Captain had hinted that she was correct – but Zanders had not said anything openly. Should she get into bed as she was now, next to Zanders' sleeping warmth? It was tempting. And The Golden Sea Captain wanted to be honest with the woman who had travelled so far and who seemed so open. But it was dangerous. The Golden Sea Captain sighed and began to dress. If she had to disguise herself in order to live the life she wanted, so be it.

Zanders was resting before the journey to Tierra de Flores, but her mind was racing. To return to her own place and time was something she'd assume would happen automatically. It had helped calm her all the months she'd been aboard The Giantess, but the Bird Woman had raised the possibility that it might not happen. In some ways, she was homesick to the point of despair, but she did not miss the body she had there, the constant, crippling pain of her injured back that so restricted her.

The injury had been meted out deliberately.

It was a crush injury, caused by the man who'd claimed to love her. Whenever out in public, his arm would reach around her shoulders, his hand gripping her tightly, pushing her down as he kept control of her movements. Years of this treatment had eventually crushed three of her lower vertebrae. The man was long gone but the damage remained. Would she have a choice as to whether to return to it?

When the landscape began to change, they knew they were close to the village. Arriving on a plateau, the pair found the land carpeted in flowers of every colour and description. Zanders had a moment of motion sickness as they waded through the undulating mass; the heat and the fifteen or so miles they'd walked beyond the end of the railway line was arduous and she was overwhelmed at the prospect of arriving at Tierra de Flores. It felt like another terminus of sorts.

That night they slept amongst the flowers. Zanders had wanted to push on – the village couldn't be far away – but they were both exhausted. At the sight of a river winding through the flowered plateau, The Golden Sea Captain suggested that they bivouac on its bank, and after drinking their fill of the icy water they lay down and slept.

The Golden Sea Captain awoke during the night; someone was nearby. He struggled for wakefulness. The plateau was lit by a million stars and he could see a shape moving towards them. Certain that it was one of the villagers, he was about to challenge the person but couldn't speak; the way the figure moved wasn't humanlike. It stood on two legs but walked as if it was used to moving on four. The Golden Sea Captain found the comforting coldness of his pistol, sat up and crossed himself.

And the creature turned and walked away.

The Golden Sea Captain handed over his gun a little reluctantly.

The villagers had known they were approaching, and that they posed no threat; an extremely elderly woman had been sitting on a boulder at the village entrance, while she rocked a baby to sleep in her arms, waiting for them. The scene was reminiscent of one of the women in Kensal, the city of the dead. Now, seated in the middle of the village – a scattering of basic buildings with a circle of rocks at its centre – The Golden Sea Captain explained to one of the village elders the reason for their visit. Zanders couldn't follow the conversation, but she saw everyone's face brighten at the mention of the *Mujer de Aves*. At the centre of the rock circle, a pot stood over a waning fire. The elder scooped up three cups of the simmering brew and they drank together. It had a similar taste to the leaves the Bird Woman had provided and she tried to prepare herself for whatever would happen next.

The Golden Sea Captain was also prepared. He had guessed that yage had been to blame for the scene at the Bird Woman's home. He had heard tales of yage, of people liberated or ruined after ingesting the plant. It seemed to suit Zanders – and the Bird Woman was clearly a veteran of the hallucinogen – and he was nervous about the effect it would have on him, but curious as well, so he sipped the brew as he translated between the elder and Zanders.

It was Zanders who first noticed how the gap between the elder's speech and the Captain's translation was narrowing. It was as if the Captain was anticipating the elder's replies. Their voices synchronised, then the elder stopped talking and drank his yage while The Golden Sea Captain talked – in English, but in the elder's voice.

"You have told me that you seek Lorena Alvarez. But does she seek you? The spirits are not our servants. Her spirit wanders the plateau although her body rests far away. I will speak with her. Would you like to meet your living relatives?"

The day had been a revelation. After the elder had disappeared into his house with more of the yage brew, Zanders met two of Lorena Alvarez's great-grandnephews. They knew of the relative who'd married an Englishman and never returned, although one spoke of seeing her ghost in the village. By nightfall, Zanders' head was whirling.

As they settled down by the fire, The Golden Sea Captain asked for his pistol to be returned – they were, after all, going to be sleeping out in the open – but was told there was no need; the village guardian would keep them safe from predators.

"I wonder if that's what I saw last night," The Golden Sea Captain said, when he and Zanders were alone. Zanders looked alarmed at the Captain's description.

"It sounds like a Werewolf!" she exclaimed, and refused to talk any more about it.

The Golden Sea Captain tried to remain awake and keep watch, but the yage had made him drowsy, and he fell asleep. When he awoke, the creature was there again. It was bent over Zanders' sleeping shadow, on all fours this time.

Feeling The Golden Sea Captain's eyes on it, it stood upright again. It was too dark to see the details of its face, but The Golden Sea Captain could feel it glaring at him. Perhaps Zanders was right and it was a Werewolf. How could this be the village guardian? It was more like a creature from Hell. It leaned over Zanders again and The Golden Sea Captain was suddenly strongly aware of not having his pistol to hand. The creature reached down and the Captain sprang to his feet.

"No!" he shouted.

The creature held up its hand, the gigantic spider that it had removed from Zanders' hair just visible in the firelight. The flickering flames made the creature's eyes glitter and illuminated a hint of a muzzle.

Zanders woke up at the sound of the Captain's voice.

"It's nothing," he said. "Just a dream."

Zanders knew he was lying and looked around. Together they watched the creature retreat.

The Golden Sea Captain sighed as his pistol was returned to him. Successful as the mission had been, Lorena Alvarez had not appeared to Zanders. The elder emerged from his home. He gave Zanders a respectful bow and spoke to The Golden Sea Captain.

"I spoke at length with Lorena Alvarez. She is close by. She is watching."

"I saw something last night," said The Golden Sea Captain. "I wasn't sure if it was a human or an animal."

The elder smiled. "The guardian is both, and more. It is a Shapeshifter."

The Golden Sea Captain crossed himself. "How can it be protecting you? A Shapeshifter is an evil entity."

"Shapeshifting is necessary sometimes," said the elder, "it is neither good nor bad. You, too, are a Shapeshifter, in certain ways."

It was said without judgment, but The Golden Sea Captain broke out in goose pimples all the same.

They didn't speak until they came to the place on the riverbank where they'd camped. Zanders, boiling over with the heat and the emotion of the visit, discarded her sticky clothes and slipped into the cool water. The Golden Sea Captain hesitated. Was it time to trust? He hoped so. He took off his clothes and, transformed, she dived into the lake.

Zanders said nothing, but, to the Captain's relief, she smiled. They didn't stay in the water for long and checked each other for leeches when they got out. As they sat on the riverbank to dry off, The Golden Sea Captain asked how long Zanders had been aware of her true identity.

"Almost straight away," said Zanders. "But I had an advantage – I've read about people like you in books. You're noted in history."

The Golden Sea Captain closed her eyes. Even having known Zanders for some time, it was dizzying to comprehend when she had come from. But her years at sea had opened her eyes to many things and the knowledge that there were other women like her – and that they were known far into the future – was something she was amazed by.

Now would be a good time to ask the Captain about her name, thought Zanders. Would it spoil things to know? To discover her birth name? It might make her seem less extraordinary. After a heavy pause, Zanders left the question unasked.

There was a six-hour wait for the train back to the coast. They found a shady spot and slept for a few hours. Back in his uniform, The Golden Sea Captain filled his water bottle from a stream and they made their way to the station, grateful to find a waiting room that was a little darker and cooler than the rest of the building. Shortly after they arrived, a colourfully dressed woman entered the room. The Captain jumped up and offered her his seat. He stood a respectful distance away and it took him a while to realise that Zanders was gesticulating at him and staring at the woman.

It was Lorena Alvarez.

Zanders felt the room get colder and wondered if it was because a ghost was there or whether it was just the chill of her own excitement. She had seen The Golden Sea Captain's gentlemanly gesture – they were sitting on the least rickety of the chairs – but had only really looked at the woman when she sat next to her and the cold had settled upon her.

The woman was looking back at her. Zanders had never seen a ghost before – she'd never seen or felt the presence of the ghost crew on The Giantess – and hadn't known what to expect. The dead who lived in Kensal had been hideous. This vision of her ancestor was different, like a trick of the light; threads woven together then splitting apart. The image of Lorena Alvarez smiled warmly. The chair creaked as she settled onto it. Or was that only in Zanders' imagination?

"You seek out the company of the dead," she said. "Are you so tired of the living?"

Zanders wanted to cry. "I've lost so much. So many people. I've nothing inside me now except pain."

"Is there no joy in your life, girl?" asked Lorena Alvarez. "You've seen with your own eyes that existence continues after death, in many different ways. All your loved ones are Elsewhere now. Some are like me, content to stay in the land of their birth. Others roam the world, some travel to the stars. This should make you happy, for they are not gone."

"They're gone from me!" Zanders barked. The words bounced off the walls and back to her.

Lorena Alvarez remained calm. Unable to comfort her, she nodded her thanks when The Golden Sea Captain crouched beside Zanders and put his arm around her.

"You came here to find me and you succeeded. You found living relatives."

"They're dead in my time," said Zanders.

"This *is* your time," The Golden Sea Captain reminded her. "And the time you came from will have their descendants in it."

Lorena Alvarez reached up and picked something from the air. "You wish to return?"

Zanders nodded slowly. "Yes…I don't know. I assumed I wouldn't have any choice now I've done what I came here to do."

Lorena Alvarez paused before speaking; long enough for them all to know that Zanders had choices.

"You will need to cross the Golden Sea."

The Golden Sea Captain's eyes widened.

"The Golden Sea? I wasn't sure it existed… it's where I've always wanted to go."

At last, thought Zanders; *the meaning behind the name.*

Lorena Alvarez was holding a chart. As she unrolled it, the sun shone through the window and Zanders had to shield her eyes from the dazzling blue and gold reflecting off the paper. When she moved her hand away from her face, The Golden Sea Captain was blocking much of the view and Lorena Alvarez was explaining something in Spanish, directions to the Golden Sea.

The Golden Sea Captain's excitement was obvious. Zanders watched him, taking the chart from Lorena Alvarez with reverence. As it passed from her hand to his, it took on a little more substance. He rolled it up and slipped it into his jacket.

"The train will be here soon," he said, almost apologetically.

Zanders wished for more time. It was always about time. She addressed Lorena Alvarez once more. "You were buried in Salcombe. Why did you stay there? You were happier here, weren't you?"

Lorena Alvarez tried to take her hand. It felt like cool air passing through it, but Zanders appreciated the gesture.

"I always meant to come home. I loved my husband but England was cold. Tuberculosis took me from him and our two children, but it brought me home. There is a reason for everything, you see; even death. One day it will come for you, too. Take comfort in that if you need to. Until then – live!"

A shrieking whistle announced the train's arrival. The threads that made up Lorena Alvarez broke up and were taken by the wind. And Zanders was crushed by loss again.

"I wish I knew what was happening at home," said Zanders. "Is anyone looking for me? Missing me?"

Peru was on the horizon now. Zanders had cried when they'd boarded The Giantess, such was the affinity she now felt for the country. They were heading towards the Golden Sea and it was time to discuss Zanders leaving.

"Would it make a difference? To you returning?"

"There won't be many who've noticed I'm gone," said Zanders. There was no self-pity in her voice; it was simply a statement of fact. "And I'm not sure how much I have to return to. But I've learnt so much about my past – things might be different now."

"I think this was meant to be," said The Golden Sea Captain. "If you hadn't arrived to take us on this mission, I might never have found someone who knew where to find the Golden Sea."

The Giantess was heading back the way they'd approached Peru. Zanders wondered how they'd find a place she'd never heard of.

"What is the Golden Sea? Why did you name yourself after it?"

The Golden Sea Captain ordered one of the ghost crew to take the wheel, and he walked with Zanders to the bow of the ship.

"I've heard things about it since I was a child. Whispers, rumours. We lived in Southampton. The docks are exciting for a child. I used to hide amongst the freight; a lot can be learned from people who don't think they're being overheard. There were men who'd crossed all the oceans of the world, faced terrible things, who wouldn't travel the Golden Sea. I never heard why, but there were hints of monsters, things that could drive you insane, in the waters there. But I also heard a woman dismissing those stories and describing it as the most beautiful place on Earth. And I knew I had to go to sea and find it."

The Golden Sea Captain paused. "We could face anything. But we both have reason to go there. So we must go."

Much as The Golden Sea Captain needed to see the Golden Sea, he was aware that it would signal the end of his travels with Zanders. When she went home then he would be alone with his ghost crew, without a mission. The past few months, culminating in the swim in the river with Zanders, had forced him to reconsider his identity. It was not so simple now; the ambition to go to sea was unthinkable until the idea of dressing as male had come about. Not just as male, but as a high ranking officer. The Golden Sea Captain was a fiction that had become more real over the years, but until Zanders had appeared, it was still only a facade. Now The Golden Sea Captain felt as one with both identities, as a Captain that was simultaneously male and female. It was no longer a choice between the two. Zanders was perfectly accepting of this duality, as the Bird Woman and the elder in Tierra de Flores had been. Perhaps it was time to be more open, more defiant, to be worthy of being written about in the history books.

He didn't want Zanders to leave.

Zanders was mulling over her conversation with Lorena Alvarez. To have found her ancestor, separated from her by time and death, was nothing short of miraculous. To be able to move freely in a body that was no longer wracked with pain was another miracle. It was wonderful but disorientating. And home was full of familiarity. Even the unpleasant sureties were reassuring in their own ways. Would Lorena Alvarez make contact again, wherever she chose to go?

"I met her and I went blank. There's so much more I wanted to know," said Zanders, breaking the silence.

"There's always more we could have done, more we want to say," said The Golden Sea Captain. "These are the things we have to live with."

Zanders looked the Captain in the eye. If she didn't go home, would he let her stay here, on The Giantess? Was it possible to be happy? The thought of such a thing almost choked her and she pushed it away.

She was woken by the Captain shaking her urgently.

"We're approaching the Golden Sea. You must see it!"

Zanders roused herself from a dream that had been about discovering a manuscript, handwritten by a much loved, dead friend; a novel with the most melancholic illustrations decorating the text. Following The Golden Sea Captain onto the deck, they hurried to the bow.

It was a moonless night, with clouds obscuring much of the starlight, but the water ahead was so bright Zanders imagined the Sun had dropped into the sea. The dark waters they were presently in were almost invisible. Zanders' stomach lurched at the sudden sensation that The Giantess was hanging in empty space. The Golden Sea Captain was trembling. It brought Zanders back to herself, and she put her arm around him. This was his moment, his life's ambition shining in the darkness.

"You know that this could be the death of both of us?" he said. "There are only stories, myths and rumours about what's actually here."

"I don't think Lorena Alvarez would have sent us here if we had no hope of crossing," said Zanders.

Strands of golden water stretched towards them, drawing them closer. This, they both knew, was going to be like nothing they'd experienced before. And they'd seen so much. As The Giantess crossed the first slivers of gold, the water beneath it bubbled. Something was rising from the depths.

The bow of The Giantess rose and slapped back down into the water as the maelstrom hit. Zanders caught sight of a huge shape, lit from within by a blue-white light, rising from the sea before she was thrown backwards. She looked up to see The Golden Sea Captain hanging on to a rope, the shape towering over him. Its six arms swirled around, threatening the ship. It looked to Zanders like a sea god, something from an ancient Greek legend, and the light inside its body gave it a gelatinous appearance, suggesting that it spent most of its life deep in the ocean. A hole opened in its head and what sounded like a voice boomed angrily out, in a language neither of the pair had heard before. Before Zanders could make sense of what it was saying, the creature exploded. She turned away, expecting to be splattered with blood and flesh, but turned back at the sound of knives scratching upon wood.

The 'sea god' was not one beast. It had been made up of a thousand creatures clinging onto one another, which were hurled in all directions. Zanders rolled away from one that swept a tentacle at her. She caught sight of The Golden Sea Captain, his face covered in scratches, waving a sword at two of the creatures.

The ship shuddered to a dead stop. Zanders picked herself up, ran to the bow and leaned over to see what had stopped it. A face was looking up at her. It was the figurehead, a mixture of anger and concern on her wooden face. As Zanders watched, she wriggled free of the bow and climbed up and aboard the ship.

And she was growing. The original carving was slightly shorter than Zanders, but untethered, the naked woman rapidly grew until she was twenty feet high.

The Golden Sea Captain had run one of the creatures through with his sword. The Giantess dismissed the other with a swipe of her hand. The ship shook as she ran around the deck, crushing some of the creatures underfoot, picking off those unwise enough to fling themselves onto her and spinning them into the sea.

Zanders had never had a physical fight in her life and she knew she'd only make things worse for the others if any of the creatures attacked her, so she found a hiding place and made herself as small as possible. The battle was short but intense, the ship rocking dangerously with the Giantess' movements. The Golden Sea Captain, bleeding now from cuts all over his arms, had killed several of the creatures but it was The Giantess who cleared the decks of the invaders. Some jumped back into the sea rather than face her. Soon it was just the three of them. Zanders emerged from her hiding place, next to the corpse of one of the creatures. It was almost translucent, the luminescence inside its body fading now it was dead. Careful to avoid its razor-sharp suckers, The Golden Sea Captain picked it up by one of its tentacles and dropped it overboard.

"I'd cook them, only I'm not sure the meat wouldn't poison us," he said between gasps for breath.

Zanders hugged him. "Thank God you're alright," she said.

The ship rocked as The Giantess walked past them to the bow. The Golden Sea Captain turned to her and thanked her for her help. She gave a drooling smile and climbed back to her place at the front of the ship as they crossed into the Golden Sea.

"She's helped me before," The Golden Sea Captain said. "The ghost crew are not able to fight."

They were below decks in the Captain's quarters. His cuts had all been cleaned but were clearly painful. He took another swig from a bottle of port.

"You should pour that on your wounds," said Zanders. "You can't risk getting them infected. What were those creatures?"

The Golden Sea Captain passed her the bottle. "Guardians, maybe, of the Golden Sea. Or something that thought of itself as a guardian. Or something far less noble – there's talk of all kinds of fabulous cargo crossing this sea." After a moment's silence, he continued. "I would bet that you're looking forward to going home now."

Zanders had a swig of port. "The Bird Woman was right. I understand what she was saying now. I can already *feel* home, that I'll be able to slip back there – or forwards, rather –when we get to the other side. Life there is easier in a lot of ways. But it's empty and it's painful. I miss home. But I don't know how I could leave this place behind."

She was close to tears now. The Golden Sea Captain put his wounded arms around her.

"It will take some time to cross the Golden Sea," he said. "By the time we get to the other side, you'll know what you want to do. Stay here with me, if it pleases you, and I'll teach you how to swordfight."

They were both exhausted but were too drawn to the Golden Sea to sleep yet. The Captain put on his shirt and they went out on deck. Icebergs were visible now, despite the warmth of the waters. This was a place of contradiction. Of possibility. The sky had cleared and the Milky Way lay like a river above them. Zanders imagined The Giantess sailing along it, the Earth a blue disc far below. She couldn't remember the last time she had imagined anything that wasn't full of sadness, and a hint of a smile broke out on her face.

Julie Travis' 'transgenre' fiction has been published in the independent press in the UK and North America for the last twenty-five years. After playing bass guitar in several punk bands, she co-founded the Queeruption international festival, has been an occasional album photographer for avant-garde band UNIT and recently co-founded Dead Unicorn Ventures, an LGBT+ events company in West Cornwall that has just published issue 1 of its zine, Dykes Ink, and held its debut event. Find her at www.julietravis.wordpress.com.

150/2020
8/5

Lightning Source UK Ltd.
Milton Keynes UK
UKHW011142131019
351525UK00005B/136/P

9 781908 125873